LIBRARIES NI
WITHDRAWN FROM STOCK

D0569626

Tips for Reading Together

Children learn best when reading is fun.

- Talk about the title and the pictures on the cover.
- Look through the pictures together so your child can see what the story is about.
- Read the story to your child, placing your finger under the words as you read.
- Have fun finding the hidden grasshopper.
- Read the story again and encourage your child to join in.
- Give lots of praise as your child reads with you.

Children enjoy reading stories again and again. This helps to build their confidence.

Have fun!

Find the grasshopper hidden in every picture.

Picnic Time

Cynthia Rider • Alex Brychta

OXFORD
UNIVERSITY PRESS

"Picnic time!" said Dad.

Biff sat on a log.

Some sheep came.

"Run!" said Kipper.

They sat on a bridge.

Some ducks came.

"Run!" said Chip.

They sat on a wall.

Some donkeys came.

"Run!" said Biff.

They sat on a rock.

Oh no! The rain came!

Think about the story

Tangled lines

Who will get the picnic?

Useful common words repeated in this story and other books at Level 1.

came on said they

Names in this story: Dad Biff Chip Kipper

More books for you to enjoy

Level 1: Getting Ready

Level 2: Starting to Read

Level 3: Becoming a Reader

Level 4: Building Confidence

Level 5: Reading with Confidence

OXFORD
UNIVERSITY PRESS
Great Clarendon Street,
Oxford OX2 6DP

Text © Cynthia Rider 2006
Illustrations © Alex Brychta 2006

First published 2006
All rights reserved

Series Editors: Kate Ruttle, Annemarie Young

British Library Cataloguing in Publication Data available

ISBN–13: 978-019-279225-9

10 9 8 7 6 5 4 3 2 1

Printed in China by Imago